SWIMMER

**Other Apple paperbacks
you will enjoy:**

SWIMMER

Harriet May Savitz

AN
APPLE®
PAPERBACK

SCHOLASTIC INC.
New York Toronto London Auckland Sydney

This book was written
for David Blatstein
by his Aunt Harriet

ISBN 0-590-33946-X

12 11 10 9 8 7 6 5 4 3 2 1   9   6 7 8 9/8 0 1/9

Printed in the U.S.A.   28

SWIMMER

1

If I tell you about Swimmer and me, then I have to tell you how Swimmer came into my life. It was just about the same time my father went out of it.

It was in June, just after my tenth birthday. One morning, my parents sat on the edge of my bed and I knew, even before they said anything, that it was bad news. I had a feeling I was going to have to be a man about it, and I wasn't sure I was ready.

"I'm leaving, Skippy." My father was crying, and it made me uncomfortable. I began to cry, too, though I wasn't even sure why.

"Where are you going?" I asked.

"Not far away. I have an apartment on Main Street, near my office." He looked as if he was waiting for me to say something.

"You don't have to go," I answered, for suddenly Main Street seemed much farther than just six blocks away.

1

My dad took my hands and held them. "It's just not good for me here," he said. "Your mother and I can't live together anymore."

My mother covered her face, as if the words hurt her. Her body was shaking. I didn't think she wanted him to leave, either.

"How are you going to tell Paul?" I asked. My brother, Paul, was in the Navy. He was stationed in Ohio and hadn't been home in months.

My father answered. "I called him this week and we had a talk. I might fly out for a weekend so that we'll have some time together."

Dad left later that day. I stood in the driveway while he piled all his clothes, his favorite velvety red armchair, and some pots and pans into a green pickup truck and drove off, away from the beach front toward Main Street.

My mother just stood there for a long time, watching that truck disappear down the street. After a while, she turned to me.

"Well, Skippy. It's just you and me now, and this."

The "this" was the big boardinghouse that would soon be filled with people who rented the rooms for the summer. We had just moved out of the three-story house with its ten rooms, as we did every spring. We put everything that was ours in the attic. Then we moved to the small bungalow in back for the summer. Vacationers would fill up the big house for ten weeks so that they could be close to the ocean. In the fall, the ten rooms would be ours again. Most of the house was still empty, but a few of the older people who didn't have kids in school had checked in early. My mother was their landlady.

"You're going to have to help me, Skippy," my mom said, looking at me as if I were much bigger and smarter than I actually was. "We only have two more weeks to fix this place up before the season really begins."

That's when I changed into my swimsuit. I knew it was time to go down to the beach. The weather was warm enough to try the ocean. Sometimes even though the air was warm, the water was too cold, but I decided to go anyway. It was the only place I could think of to sort things out. Whenever anything important happened to me, I'd walk the one block to the boardwalk, then down the steps, across the soft sand, and take a swim. Or sometimes I'd just sit and stare at the water. The beach and the waves had a way of taking care of everything.

I had something serious for it to take care of that day. I had never thought about my father leaving. Maybe dying, but never just leaving. I hoped the sound of the ocean would help me understand why.

There was no one else around when I got to the beach. I dropped my beach towel on the sand and decided to take a swim. I knew if my dad was there, he wouldn't let me go in alone.

"Never go in without the lifeguards on duty," he'd say. "The ocean is a tricky lady. She can change on you without warning."

Dad always insisted we swim inside the ropes. You see, we live on the Jersey Shore and the waters are rough. All the beaches have roped-off areas. Poles are stuck in the sand with ropes tied from one to the other, until it looks like one big square, roped off in the water. There's always a rope to hang on and the lifeguards can keep better track of everyone who is swimming. Swimmer used to go outside the ropes until I told him why we shouldn't, and he listened.

The water around my ankles felt good. Cool, but not too cold. I dipped under real fast and began to swim back and forth inside the ropes. Back and forth. Back and forth. I thought a lot while I pushed against the ocean, and I think I cried, but I couldn't really tell. The salt water was in my eyes, and gave me a good excuse to make up for all the crying I was trying not to do in the driveway when my dad left.

The more I swam, the more my head cleared until I had to admit I knew my dad was going to leave sometime. He and my mother fought too much to be happy living in the same house. In between dipping under the waves, I thought back to all their arguments and decided it wasn't a good way for anyone to live.

My eyes stung and the afternoon sun was bright so that my eyes were nearly shut. Because I couldn't see too well, I didn't see Swimmer. I just felt him, or at least I felt something next to me, swimming along by my side. I could hear someone breathing and felt another body next to mine. It was about the second time across that I turned my head and forced my eyes open. When I finally managed to blink away the water, I was looking directly into the big brown eyes of a dog.

All I saw was his head. The rest of his body was underwater. His legs were paddling away and the faster I swam, the faster he paddled. We were going neck and neck for a long time.

It made swimming without my dad a little easier to take. After about a half hour of matching strides, I got a little tired. I guess the dog did, too, because he followed me onto the beach. I lay down on the towel and he lay on the sand beside me.

In the sun, his golden hair dried smooth and soft. It was almost the same color as mine. He was a large dog, as long as my towel when he stretched out. Now and then, he'd get up, shake himself off, then lie down again beside me.

I think we both fell asleep for a while. Finally, I had to get back to the house. Mom needed all the help she could get. As the landlady, she had to make sure all the rooms were tidy, the floors washed, and clean linens put on the beds. There was some painting to do, too. Old Jim Henley came over now and then to help us paint, but he had a bad cough and it kept him home much of the time. The work was slow in getting done, and now there was just me and Mom to do everything that needed to be done.

"I got to go, fella." When I petted the dog's wet head, I noticed he didn't have a collar on. I remember looking around to see if anyone else was on the beach. Sometimes joggers brought their dogs along to run with them, but no one seemed to be around. I thought maybe he was a winter dog who knew his way around and swam every chance he could, just like my dad and I used to.

When I got home, there was a letter from Paul waiting for me. I noticed that lately he was writing a lot. It was funny, Paul had more to say to me

now that he was living hundreds of miles away
than he did when he lived at home.

"Dear Skip," he wrote:
How you doing? I hope you get this letter
by Saturday. Dad told me he and Mom were
going to talk to you then. Listen, Skipper,
try to help Mom out. With me and Dad gone
now, you're just about all she has. I sure wish
I was around to help you, but I had to get
away. You know, I lived in that town all my
life. I never went much anywhere else, never
saw anything else, and I just had to make a
move on my own. Know what I mean? Maybe
you will when you get older.

Boy, I sure miss that ocean, Skipper.
Being stationed in the Midwest wasn't ex-
actly what I had in mind when I decided to
get away from the shore. But I hear I'll be
getting transferred soon, maybe to Califor-
nia. I sure hope that's so. I miss the smell of
that salt water.

Hey Skipper, is ole Perry coming down
again, and his father with that loud voice and
old Mrs. Patterson who was always complaining that her toilet didn't work right? Boy, I
can hear them now all the way to Ohio. I bet
Mom's real busy getting ready for the tour-

ists. She's lucky she has you with her to help her out.

I'm going to try to write Dad and Mom today, too. Take care, Skipper. And take a swim for me.

Love,
Paul

I folded the letter and put it back in the envelope. Then I placed it in the bureau drawer alongside the others I had received from Paul.

I picked up a piece of paper and began to write an answer, one of those honest letters that I usually kept to myself but now felt like letting out.

Dear Paul,

This is your brother, Skipper, answering your last letter. The ocean is great — warm and calm. (It wasn't. It was cold and rough, but I decided I wanted Paul to miss it a lot.) The air is just right and people are stretched out on their beach chairs already. (They weren't. There had been a lot of rain and everyone had been stuck inside.)

You know, Paul, I wish you wouldn't tell me how important it is for me to help Mom out now that I'm the only one here to help her. It sure would have been easier if you had stayed around. Maybe then Dad would be here, too. You know he always liked playing baseball with you after school. I never could catch that ball the way you could. But then you left, and it didn't take Dad long to leave, too. So I wish you'd stop telling me what I should do. You're not here and you left just like Dad. I think he would have stayed if you had.

Yeah, Mrs. Patterson is still yelling about the toilet. We have a new lady in the house, Mrs. Cooperson. She keeps hollering because someone keeps taking her ice cream out of the freezer in the big kitchen. She thinks it's the lady who sits next to her and the lady next to her, Mrs. Goodman, keeps yelling that Mrs. Patterson is stealing her cans of tuna fish out of the cabinets.

So nothing has changed and I hope Ohio is great and I'm sorry it doesn't have an ocean.

Love,
Skipper

I reread the letter and thought I wouldn't like to receive one like it. It was bad enough that Paul had to live without the ocean nearby. I ripped it up and decided to write him when I had something nice to say. But the way things were going around here, that might not be for a long time.

2

I didn't get down to the beach during the week because of school and a northeaster that hit our town. It was a big storm that turned the waters churning and gray. The wind blew the water up on the boardwalk and you couldn't even walk on the boards. By the end of the week, the weather had turned warm and sunny and I began missing the beach again.

I missed my dad more. He and my mother had arranged once-a-week and every-other-weekend visits. I wanted to see him more often, but they told me it wasn't good for me. I couldn't figure that out. When he was home I saw him every day and that made me feel terrific. But I went along with it because there didn't seem to be much I could do.

The first time I visited my dad on the weekend, he took me to see his apartment. It was furnished and he had all good food in the refrigerator, most of it my favorite snacks. We went to a movie together, but it wasn't like it used to be. There was something between us now. I knew that at the end of our visit he would be going one way and I would be going the other. So when the visit was over, I was ready for the beach. I could tell that ocean a bit about what was going on in my mind.

"Just an hour and then come right back," my mother told me. She was hanging bed linens out on the back line next to the bungalow and a man was working on the pool in the back of our house, getting it ready for the summer. We had the only pool in town. Even though everyone in the boarding house could bathe in the ocean, some people just liked pool swimming. And some were just too old to walk to the beach. My dad used to take care of the pool, painting it every couple of years.

The dog was swimming when I got to the beach. It was as if he was waiting for me. We went through our laps together and lay down on the sand just the way we did the last time. Only this time he licked my feet and when he finally dozed off, his wet head was resting on my stomach. It was comfortable to pet him that way.

"It's not going to be easy," I said out loud. It was late afternoon and no one was around to hear me. "I get up every morning missing my dad, and I go to sleep every night thinking he's in the next room. I can't tell Mom that because she won't talk about him. When he comes to pick me up, he has to stay outside."

The dog's ears moved as if he was listening with interest. Then one eye opened and shut again. Suddenly I realized I wasn't talking to the ocean anymore. I was talking to the dog. It was much better.

When I left him this time, it was harder to do. He walked me up to the boardwalk steps and stood there as if he was waiting for me to tell him what to do. I sort of thought he wanted to come home with me.

"Hey, fellow, I know you've got a home," I told him. "You're too pretty for anyone to let you go."

I wanted to believe that because I knew I couldn't bring him home. There was a NO PETS sign on the front of the brick wall that surrounded our boardinghouse. That sign had been there for years, and whenever any of the roomers asked if they could bring down their pets, my mother always answered, "I can't have any pets here. People walk around barefoot and I have to keep the place clean."

It had always been that way. So you see, I really wanted to believe the dog had a home and was just having a good time swimming in the ocean. I couldn't bear to think he was a stray, alone, with no home to go to.

He didn't make it easy for me. He jumped up so he was standing on his hind legs with both his front paws on my shoulders. Then he washed my face with his tongue. I hugged him back, then ran up the steps toward home.

I couldn't forget about him all night. While I was helping Mom wash the dishes and hang curtains in one of the rooms, all I could see were those big brown eyes and that golden hair. I still felt the hug.

The next morning while my mom was sleeping, I sneaked out of bed, put on my bathing suit, and ran up the block toward the beach. I gave myself the excuse that this was the last weekend before all the summer boarders came down. From now on, things would be busier than ever. I knew I would have to be home more to help Mom.

I ran down the beach, half hoping the dog wouldn't be there. I almost wished he was miles away. I pictured him sleeping in a nice safe place. I looked at the water. There was no one swimming in it. I didn't much blame them. It was rough and I wasn't going to go in, either. The waves were crashing against each other and over the tops of the ropes.

I looked both ways along the beach and didn't see the dog. That made me feel good. I knew that if he was here this time, I couldn't leave him. I was just about to take my towel and go home when I saw him. He was under the boardwalk, digging into a garbage can.

I walked over and watched him. He looked hungry and was trying to lick some scraps of cupcake off a piece of waxed paper. I took the paper out of the garbage can and helped him.

He sat down next to me. He was taller than I was when we were sitting. He looked at me for a long time, as if we both knew there was a decision coming.

I carefully went over his neck to see if there was a mark from a collar. The hair was thick and golden, but there was nothing there. No identification tags. No collar. This time when I walked up the steps to the boardwalk, he followed me, as if we had already made the decision.

We walked home together. I stopped in front of the brick wall and sat down on the sidewalk in front of the NO PETS sign.

"You know, Swimmer," I said, realizing that was the only name I could think of for him, "you can't read this sign, but it has a lot to do with what happens to you and me today."

He looked at the sign and licked it. I thought he might be thirsty.

"Stay here."

I ran around to the back of our bungalow and

14

poured some water from the outside faucet into a little plastic bowl that was sitting on one of the outdoor tables. I brought it back to him. One slurp and it was gone. I ran and got another.

Then we just sat there, the two of us, trying to figure things out. This was no time to talk to Mom about having a dog. I couldn't see her taking down that sign for anything. And with Dad just out of the house, I didn't think she would be in the mood to understand how Swimmer and I had come together, or why I felt I needed him now.

So if we were going to be together, and if Swimmer was going to be mine, since he didn't belong to anyone else, I decided I would have to keep him in a place that didn't bother the boarders or my mother. In fact, it probably would be better, I remember thinking, if no one knew about him at all.

It was then that I remembered the old abandoned house around the corner. It had been empty for a year now.

"The city bought the land but hasn't decided what to do about the house," Mom had told me last time we passed it.

It was a big house and my friends and I went over there a lot to play around the grounds. The porch was rickety and the broken windows on the first floor had been boarded up.

All but one, and I had found it. It led to the basement. One day when I was playing, I looked inside. It was dark and musty in there, with some old chairs piled up as if someone had forgotten all about them.

Well, I walked around the corner as if I was just going to old Charlie's for a morning paper for my mom. Swimmer followed me. Old Charlie had a grocery store across the street from the abandoned house. It was the only store close by for blocks. Charlie had all kinds of things to sell — groceries, newspapers, candy, and just about anything else you could think of. He also had the best ice cream sandwiches in town.

Swimmer and I walked together as if we had always been that way. Now and then he'd bump against me as if he wanted to remind me he was still there. The basement window in the abandoned house was big enough for both of us to climb in when we got there.

"Swimmer, this isn't fancy, and you look like a fancy dog. But it's dry and sort of safe," I explained as we took a good look around the basement.

Swimmer had a hungry look in his eyes as he sat there. His tongue was hanging way down and he was panting as if he was nervous. I thought he needed to be petted. I don't know if it made him feel better, but it made me feel good when I petted him.

"Stay here. I'll be right back," I said. Swimmer sat there looking at me. "Stay," I ordered, hoping he was a good listener.

Then I ran home. I picked up a plastic bowl I sometimes kept paper clips in, got some of my allowance from the wallet on my bureau, and ran over to old Charlie's for a bag of dry dog food.

"Have a dog now, Skip?" Charlie asked, getting up from the stool he always sat on behind the counter.

"No," I answered, feeling I wasn't really lying. "I'm just feeding someone else's dog." I also felt that was partly true.

I knew Charlie got all the news in town first and everyone came to his store to find out what was happening. I decided to ask if anyone was looking for a dog.

"Not that I know of," Charlie answered me. His eyebrows went up a little as if he wondered why I was asking. I decided not to stick around while he thought about it.

Before long, Swimmer had eaten two bowls of dry dog food and drunk two bowls of cold water.

"This is your home now, Swimmer — until things straighten out at my home. We have to get through the summer first."

17

I left Swimmer there sleeping. I hoped he would understand that he was safe and that he could come back to the abandoned house and find food. I wanted him to know that I wanted him with me, and that even if we couldn't live together, I'd take care of him.

The days went by quickly. Soon, the rooms in our house filled up. I hated living in the bungalow. During the winter, when we lived in the big house, there was plenty of room. I had my own bedroom and so did Paul when he was home. There was a big living room, and a kitchen that looked out on the pool with pretty plants along the windowsills.

Now the boarders had taken over our house. The summer tenants thought all those rooms belonged to them. We were squeezed into the little bungalow — one big room for everybody to sleep and eat in. We had a couple of those fold-up beds that we put in a corner when we were done with them, and there was a large hot plate to do the cooking.

As soon as we moved in, I hung a big calendar on the wall, just as you walk in the door. I started marking it off, one day at a time, with a big X through the number. I couldn't wait until I could move back into my house again in the fall.

3

It wasn't only living in the crowded bungalow that made the summer so difficult. It was the orders and the complaints. All day they just kept coming. The boarders seemed to be ordering my mother around all the time. I couldn't stand the way they talked to her sometimes.

"You mean those same garbage cans are here again this year?"

"You're raising the rent again? My friend on Second Avenue doesn't pay as much as I do."

"I don't like the curtains. Could you change them?"

"It's too hot in the kitchen. Can't you put a fan in?"

I wanted to tell them to be quiet. She was just one person. Without my father, it was all on her now. I wanted to tell them that and ask them one question, just one: If you don't like anything in our house, why do you keep coming back every summer? Some of them had been coming back for

19

five years. Actually I didn't think they would listen to anything I had to say. They were down at the shore for ten weeks of fun and they didn't want to know anything about anyone else, especially their landlady.

It wasn't only my mother they ordered about. Sometimes they came after me.

"Skip, will you pick up a newspaper for me?"

"Skip, go get your mother. I need her."

"Skip, carry this package."

"Skip, don't run around the porch. We're sleeping."

"Skip, try not to talk so loud."

It was my house, I thought. It was theirs only in the summer, yet they acted as if they owned it.

Perry Harris acted as if he owned it, too. Perry Harris always managed to ruin my summers. He was eleven years old, bigger and older than I was. He had dark black hair and the kind of eyes that never looked directly at you.

There wasn't too much I liked about Perry. He had a way of hanging around me all the time. If I was cleaning out the pool, he'd be sitting by the edge, watching me. If I was emptying out the garbage cans, he'd be walking behind me. Even when I was watching television in the big kitchen, he'd be sitting at the table, watching it, too, even though he had a television in his own room.

For the past three years, Perry and his parents had taken one of the front rooms overlooking the porch. Each year I hoped that we would get a letter telling us Perry wasn't coming down. It didn't happen. When he and his parents piled out of their car with all their suitcases and pots and pans, I knew the summer had really begun.

Perry's father was a big man. He had a loud voice and liked to use it to give orders. He only came down on weekends. When he did, you could hear his voice booming right out of their small room and into the yard.

Most of my time now was spent helping my mom. School was out for the summer and I had more time to give her. She began to pay me for some of the chores, which meant I was able to put money away for Swimmer's food.

Swimmer and I had our own schedule. We'd go swimming together early in the morning whenever the weather was nice. Sometimes he'd walk me to the brick wall. Sometimes I'd walk him to the broken window in the basement.

Old Charlie kept me supplied with dog food. "You really have a hungry dog there, Skip," he'd say. "That friend is lucky he has you to feed the dog. Is he giving you money for the dog food?"

I nodded my head, feeling no answer was better than lying. Actually it was an expensive job, feeding Swimmer. He really worked up an appetite after a day of swimming and running the beaches, scrounging under the boardwalk, and playing with some of the kids on the beach.

Sometimes I worried that he would run off, but he always returned to the basement.

When I was out on my bike one day, I found some old blankets and rugs that had been left by the side of the curb for the garbage men. I dragged them down to the basement and Swimmer really liked them. He slept on them all the time.

Between working around our house and taking care of Swimmer, I didn't have much time for Perry Harris. I didn't mind, but he did. Whenever I looked as if I had nothing to do, Perry would pull out the deck of cards he always had on him.

"Want to play war?" he'd ask. War was his favorite card game. I hated playing war and figured I had played over a thousand games with Perry during the past three summers. I had also run about a thousand errands. His mother was always nagging my mother for something and sending Perry with the messages.

The first week they were there he came over asking for more toilet paper and complaining that the ceiling light had blown out in their bedroom.

"What are you doing with all that toilet paper?" I asked, trying to sound like my father. He used to get mad when everyone started wasting the toilet paper or taking it into their rooms so that no one else could use it. "It seems all our money is going into toilet paper," he'd yell every time he had to replace it. I never understood why he got so angry, but now with Perry standing over me, I was beginning to feel that same kind of anger.

"My mom says everyone in the house is going to have to supply their own paper," I said, getting a yellow roll from under the cabinet in the kitchen. "I mean, this stuff doesn't grow on trees."

Perry smiled and it was the last thing I felt like seeing on his face. "Well it does," he said. "Sort of."

"Here's the bulb." I shoved a sixty-watt bulb at Perry, who was tossing the roll of paper up in the air looking smug.

"Mom says you should put it in. She's afraid to do stuff like that."

I looked at him, wondering if he was kidding me. "All she has to do is unscrew the old one and put this new one in," I said.

"My mother doesn't like to do things like that."

My hand tightened around the box with the bulb in it. Once, just once, I needed to tell Perry off. But I knew I couldn't. My mother would be upset

23

and she had enough to upset her without my adding to it.

I got a stepladder out of the kitchen closet and followed Perry to his apartment. We were alone there. I stood on the ladder and stretched up to unscrew the bulb while Perry held on to the ladder.

"I can get it . . . you don't have to help me." I angrily shoved his hand with my foot.

But Perry persisted. "The ladder's wiggly . . . you might lose your balance."

I wasn't in the mood to hear anything that Perry said. "There's nothing wrong with this ladder. It's a great ladder. My dad bought it."

"I didn't say there was anything wrong with the ladder," Perry protested. "I just don't want you to fall. Look, it's not my fault my mom wants these things done."

Finally the lightbulb was in place and the toilet paper on the roller. "Remember," I said, "tell your mother from now on everyone has to buy their own paper."

"Want to play cards?" were Perry's final words as I turned to leave.

"I'm too busy working around here," I answered.

I was telling the truth about that. The next

thing I had to do was mop the kitchen floor. But the kitchen was one of my favorite places to hang out. That's where everyone did their cooking and eating if they didn't have a place to cook in the rooms they rented. It was called a community kitchen. Everyone ate there together.

There was a television in the kitchen, but even better than that was the conversation in the kitchen. Sometimes they talked in front of me as if I wasn't even there. I didn't like it when they talked about each other. I couldn't imagine why they did that. They ate together, played cards together, swam in the pool together, and laughed together at night when they sat by the pool and talked. I couldn't understand why they said mean things behind each other's backs. But then I remembered the way they talked about my mother and I guessed they just had mean things to say about everybody.

That night at dinner my mom said, "Try to be nicer to Perry. They pay a good price for that room and we really need the money."

"How come?" I asked. I couldn't remember her ever saying we needed money before. Besides, now there was just the two of us. The Navy was taking care of Paul. Dad was taking care of himself.

"Your father isn't sending us enough money,"

she said. Her mouth tightened as if she didn't want to talk about it anymore. I didn't, either. I didn't want to have to have another problem to think about.

Then I thought about the letter I had been meaning to write to Paul and decided it was time to do it now. Even though there were plenty of people around, I felt sort of lonely, like I needed to sit down and talk to someone. Maybe Paul would listen.

Dear Paul,
There's an awful lot to do around here. I got to tell you, Mom and I are working hard, but the people renting the big house don't seem satisfied with anything we do.

I stopped writing for a minute, wondering if I should tell Paul about Swimmer. Even though I was getting to know him better since he was writing to me, I didn't know if he would keep it a secret. I couldn't take the chance.

The only good thing happening is the weather right now. It's sunny and I get a chance to swim just about every day in the ocean.

26

I didn't mention who I was swimming with.

I hope everything is going great in Ohio. I miss you being here.

Love,
Skipper

4

"Want to go swimming?" Perry asked.

He was sitting on one of the rocking chairs on the front porch. His face was peeling. It always did when he stayed too long in the sun. Half of it was red, and half white from the peeling skin. He was wearing his swimsuit and a white shirt on top. He always looked as if he was dressed to go to school, even when he was going swimming. Maybe because he was wearing socks and sneakers. I never did in the summer. Even now my feet were bare.

"Sure," I answered. My chores were done in the house and I now considered Perry a job that would make my mother happy. I grabbed my beach towel off the line in back of the bungalow and ran off to the beach with him.

We got into a sand fight as soon as we got there so that we both had to run in the water and get washed off. We started swimming back and forth because the water was calm. Perry was a good swimmer. There were a lot of people in the water so we had to pick a space to swim in. The two of us swam back and forth for a while. Then it was the three of us. Swimmer had joined us and was on my side. If a dog could smile, he was smiling. His mouth was spread from side to side and his white teeth showed.

I pretended I didn't know he was there. But Perry stood up, his hands on his sides, his dark eyes open wide.

"Look at that dog," he sputtered. "He's swimming and keeping up with us."

"How do you like that," I said, looking around as if I was bored.

Swimmer stopped swimming, too. He just sort of doggie paddled in one place in the water with that big smile on his face.

"He looks like he knows you," Perry said, petting Swimmer's head. I wanted him to keep his hands off my dog, but I didn't say anything. I kept remembering that NO PETS sign on the front wall of our house, and the summer Perry's mother asked if she could bring down their cat.

"I can't let you do it," my mother had insisted.

"But I'll have to board her at the vet on weekends," Perry's mother had whined.

"I'm sorry. If I do it for you, I'll have to do it for everyone else," my mother had answered. Once she made up her mind to something, she stuck to it.

I remembered that cat. I knew I could not let Perry find out about Swimmer. Not for anything. It hurt me to do it, but I had to do it for Swimmer's own good.

"Go home," I said sternly. I was hoping he would remember where home was.

Swimmer gave me one of those long looks, his head sort of tilted to one side, as if he was thinking over my order. Then he swam off to the edge of the water and ran up on the beach.

I thought he was listening, but he wasn't. He waited, and followed Perry and me to the towel and watched as we tried to build one of those sand castles near the water. Every time we got the thing built, a wave came up and knocked it down. Swimmer tried to help by digging into the sand with his paws as if he had figured out the game.

"Boy, he sure is a friendly dog," Perry said. "He acts as if he knows you."

Perry said this because Swimmer was giving me one of his hugs, the kind with both paws on my shoulders.

I shoved him aside. "Go home," I whispered in his ear. He licked my face and sat down on our castle.

"Well, I guess that's the end of that," Perry said.

We walked home with Swimmer following us.

"Do you think he expects to come home with us?" Perry asked, petting Swimmer now and then.

I shrugged my shoulders. "Maybe he lives on the same block."

When we got to the wall in front of our boardinghouse, I said, "Go home," straightening my shoulders as I gave the command. I put out my hand and pointed in the direction of the abandoned house. "Home," I said again.

Swimmer jumped up, hugged me one more time, and then went on his way. I knew he was probably expecting his supper, so I told Perry I had to go in and help my mom. Then I ran to the bungalow, got some money for a new bag of dog food, and ran over to Charlie's.

It was beginning to cost me a lot to feed Swimmer. I was lucky that Mom was paying me extra to clean the pool in the morning. I'd take one of those long hoses and vacuum out the leaves. There was a net I used for that, too. Then sometimes I'd help Mom put the chemicals into the pool so that the water would be clean. Whatever she paid me was going toward Swimmer's food, with a little left over for the penny arcade on the boardwalk.

Charlie had a faucet outside in back of his store, where I filled Swimmer's water bowl.

"That dog of yours sure can eat," Charlie said as I carried the bag of dog food out of the store. "How long is your friend going to be gone?"

The reason Charlie knew all the news in town was because he was always asking questions. "For the summer," I said, realizing I did not intend to end my friendship with Swimmer.

He was waiting for me outside the house, lying in the sun by the basement window. His tail wagged as soon as he saw me. I fed him outside in the sun. I wasn't worried about anyone seeing us. There were five big trees circling the house, and bushes all around the grounds protecting it. From the street, you could just see the very top floor.

I watched Swimmer eat. It was funny, but it made me feel good just taking care of him. Since my dad left, there was an emptiness inside me. It was with me all the time, the kind of feeling you get when you're hungry. But eating didn't fill it up. With Swimmer next to me, I didn't feel as empty.

When Swimmer was finished eating, I went into the basement with him. I put the bag of dog food high up on a shelf where he couldn't reach it.

"I wish I had a nicer place for you to stay,

Swimmer," I told him, stroking his golden hair. "You're so pretty. You deserve the best place of all."

The best place, I was thinking, was at the foot of my bed or sleeping on the rug in my bedroom. But I knew that couldn't be. I looked over my shoulder now and then as I left. Swimmer was sleeping soundly. He slept sounder than anyone I knew. I didn't like leaving him there. Each morning when I came to pick him up to go swimming, I worried that he wouldn't be there. I wasn't sure he knew he was mine.

The month of July went by slowly. Usually at the beginning of the summer my mother was raring to go. But with my father gone, she didn't have that power she used to have. She didn't laugh as much or jump out of bed as quickly as she once did. The people who were renting the rooms seemed to sense she wasn't herself. Some of them felt sorry for her.

"I heard her husband left her," I overheard Mrs. Patterson say one day while I was watering the flowers by the side of the house.

Some of the boarders just didn't care. "Things certainly aren't as pleasant around here as they were last year," Mrs. Johnson complained. "I don't know why we have to suffer because she's unhappy. The bathrooms are not as clean as they used to be."

I wanted to tell them it was probably because I was cleaning them. My mother couldn't do everything herself. I wanted to tell them how hard it was for her now. But I was afraid. I knew my mother depended on them for her income, money that would help us get through the winter. I didn't want to spoil that. But it wasn't fair.

One of the boarders called her every night after dinner with a complaint. Just as my mom was putting up her feet after supper, the phone would ring.

"Mrs. Apple," Mom would say wearily, going to the phone. "What does she want fixed now?"

Most of the time, Mrs. Apple wanted things fixed right away. Then my mother would get up from her chair, pick up the toolbox, and go out front to the big house.

I hurt inside for her then. The next time I saw my father, I told him what was going on. A strange look crossed his face, as if he didn't want to hear.

"Don't worry about it, Skip. Your mother will manage," he said. Then he took me for an ice cream sundae.

I loved hot fudge sundaes. But that night, it didn't taste quite so good. I wanted him to tell me he would help Mom, maybe come over and help her the way he used to after his work at the office. I wanted him to tell me he wasn't happy being away from us. I wanted him to tell me he'd be at breakfast in the morning and next to me swimming, and all of the other things we used to do together.

He didn't talk much that night and I left part of my sundae in the bowl.

It wasn't good when I came home from my father, either. My mother always had a sad look on her face when I came through the door. Sometimes, when my dad dropped me off, I saw her looking through the window, peeking by the side of the curtain as if she didn't want anyone to see her.

"How did things go?" she would ask.

I don't know how she expected them to go. I always said, "Okay." But later I would hear her talking to Dad on the telephone and her voice was hard, angry, the way it used to be during their fights in the kitchen.

"I don't want you to see him too often," she'd say into the telephone. "He's unhappy when he comes home. It's hurting him too much."

Then sometimes she'd say, "How could you do this to us? Just because you weren't happy. Who said you had to be happy?"

Now that I think about it, I don't remember Dad being too happy for a long time before he left, maybe a year or two. He seemed extra grumpy and he'd sit in that red velvety chair for a long time, just staring out the big window in the front of our living room. His eyes would grow sad, and he would sigh as if he saw something terrible.

I never saw it. I looked out the same window and all I could ever see was a big maple tree, a parking lot across the street, and a small apartment house behind it. I wondered why he wasn't happy. I thought about it a lot, but I never could figure it out.

Whenever I felt sad, I headed for the beach. I could think better there and I could always find something to do. There were shells to collect and sand castles to build. Sometimes it was just fun walking under the boardwalk, collecting pieces of wood. But the ocean was the best fun of all. If I wasn't in it, I was watching it. The fishermen's boats were always there, and the seagulls never went away.

5

Just about everything that could go wrong went wrong that month of July. Two chairs were stolen from the pool patio. The plumbing broke down in Mrs. Goodman's apartment, and Mr. Jasper, who always sat rocking on the front porch, got stung by a bee and was rushed to the hospital. He was okay, but he insisted that Mom should have sprayed better and so she had to do it all over again. Mrs. Apple, who always vacuumed to keep her place extra clean and had two television sets and an air-conditioner in her apartment, blew the fuses about twice a week. Then everyone in the house lost their electricity.

I kept crossing off each day on the calendar. Even though it was only July, Mom looked as tired as if it was September. I think we both wished by then that it was fall. Every day the suggestion box hanging by the front door of our bungalow was filled to the top with notes.

I helped all I could but deep down inside, something was missing from me, too. I missed my dad. I didn't know which was worse — the fights in the house and watching him sit by the window, or just knowing he was up on Main Street but no longer a part of our family. Each time I left him, I couldn't believe he wasn't coming home.

But having Swimmer helped. It was getting better and better when we swam each morning. It was the best time of the day for both of us. The morning was fresh, the sky clear blue, the beach soft and clean and empty. The two of us had the water practically to ourselves. I'd make sure we stayed close to the beach and away from the really deep water. Back and forth we'd go, with Swimmer spreading that big smile when we finished.

He always insisted on walking me to my house. No matter how I tried to convince him to turn the corner before we got there, he'd walk beside me. Then he'd give me one last hug before he left. It made me nervous because sometimes Perry was out on the porch by the time we got home, and I could almost feel his curious eyes on us.

You see, I just wasn't sure about Perry being a friend. If he had company from the city and anyone would ask who I was, Perry would tell them I was his friend. But I never said that. I didn't really feel it. There was something about

38

Perry that made me think if I was in trouble, he wouldn't be there to help me. Not like Pete and Billy, my very best friends. Pete was away at his grandmother's for the summer and Billy went to camp all summer. I would have told them about Swimmer if they were here. I could tell them anything.

But I thought if Perry found out about Swimmer, and about me feeding the dog, he wouldn't keep it to himself. He would probably tell his mother, who would tell my mother, who would put an end to my spending money on Swimmer's food. She would probably call the animal shelter and that would be that.

So I didn't tell Perry and I tried to keep out of his way as much as I could. And of course I never let Swimmer come to our house.

"I'm busy working on the pool," I'd say to Perry if he asked me to go fishing at Star Lake on the small bridge that went from our town to the next.

"I have to wash the floors," I'd tell him when he wanted to go to the amusement park in Sandy City, just a few blocks down the boardwalk.

Swimmer was my only friend now. He was bringing all kinds of gifts back to the abandoned house. One day he brought a big red sun hat he must have found on the beach. It was waiting in the basement. Another time, he found an old glove.

He'd slap it around when he played with me, throwing it up in the air and waiting for me to try to catch it. Then when I'd grab for it, Swimmer would pull in the other direction, wagging his tail. I got the feeling that Swimmer knew this was his real home now and he was furnishing it. There were a few old meat bones lying around. One day, he brought home a tennis ball.

That was the best gift of all. Swimmer and I would play ball in the backyard. Whenever I threw the ball, he'd catch it. I couldn't help thinking how proud my father would have been of him. I almost wished Swimmer could teach me how to catch. Maybe if I practiced, I'd get better. Maybe if I got better, my dad would move back. Swimmer and I began to play a lot of ball.

But it didn't do any good. My dad moved, but he didn't move back to our house. He moved to another city, in another state. One morning my mother received a phone call.

"Bob," she said, "you're moving so far away. What will Skip do?"

I sat outside, under the open window, where I could hear everything. There was a long, quiet time. Then she said, "But I need him here during the summer. You know that. He's all the help I have."

I heard her crying. Then her voice got angry. "I don't care if you hated this town. I don't care if you're not happy. What about us?"

The phone was slammed down. I knew I had to talk this over with Swimmer. I ran to the basement, hoping he would be there. He wasn't, so I sat there myself on his rug, throwing his tennis ball up and down. Finally he came in. He was surprised to see me because it wasn't his meal-time. His tail wagged and he gave me one of those toothy grins.

I petted his head and he sort of folded up and lay half on my lap, half on the rug. I wasn't planning on crying, but my face felt wet. Sometimes you just have to have someone to cry with. Swimmer seemed to understand. He kept licking off the tears, making room for more. Thinking back on that day, I guess it was the most miserable day of my life.

I didn't realize how much it meant to me, having Dad on Main Street. Even though he wasn't living at home anymore, he wasn't that far away. I knew if I timed it right, I could always see him in the diner having his lunch, or drop into the office if I needed him. I guess I didn't tell him that I needed him, but I thought he knew it.

Anyway, it wouldn't have made a difference. If

he wasn't happy in this town, he was going to move out.

"You know, Swimmer, I'll never leave you like that. I promise." I squeezed him real good so he'd believe me. Then I went back home.

"Your dad is moving to New York City," my mother told me. Her eyes were really red and she kept blowing her nose. I guess my eyes were red, too, but she didn't notice.

"Why couldn't we go, too?" I asked. That's what I couldn't understand. He didn't have to be happy here. But I knew I could have been happy in New York City or anywhere else with him, as long as we were together.

I wasn't sure about my mother. She had been born here. "I can't be far from the ocean," she had once said. But I didn't think that would stop her if all of us could be happy together.

We sat down at the kitchen table. There was room in the little bungalow for a small kitchen table, four chairs, a tiny sink and refrigerator, and the fold-away cots.

"Skip. It isn't that simple. Your dad didn't want us with him." She said it as if the words hurt. Then she changed her mind. "He didn't want *me* with him," she said.

"Did he want me?" I asked. I sure felt he did.

Then I began to think of all the things I had done to get him angry. The list grew longer. Maybe he was unhappy because I didn't take the garbage out when he asked. Or there was the time I busted his good fishing rod.

"He wanted you," my mother said. She had her arm around me. "He wants you with him now. But I need you, Skip. Not just here to help with the house. I need you for me. With your father gone, you're all I have. Do you understand?"

I didn't. I felt like one of those rubber bands when you pull each end and stretch it. They both wanted me. That made me feel good. But I couldn't be with both of them, not anymore, not with my dad moving from Main Street. That didn't make me feel so good at all.

"He feels he could take just as good care of you as I do," my mom continued. She got up and took some grapes from the refrigerator. They were cold and juicy. Eating them kept my stomach from tumbling all about.

"I don't think he can," she went on. "He's got to go to work every day. He's got a new job in the city." She was chewing the grapes very slowly, as if she wasn't hungry at all. Then she looked at me. "I told him I wouldn't let him have you."

I felt like the old lamp my father wanted to take

the day he left. "I bought it," he shouted at my mother, grabbing the lamp.

"But it belongs to our house. You just can't go around the house taking what you want," Mom had yelled back. They were both clutching the lamp as if it were made of gold. Finally Dad let go. I felt sorry for that old lamp.

I felt that someone was clutching me now. I wanted them to let me go. I put the grapes down on the kitchen table and went outside. Mom followed me.

"Perry's mother was upset yesterday, Skip. She said you're not playing with him anymore and he doesn't have any other friends here. You know how important it is that they be happy here. I need them to come back next year. Please be nice to Perry."

My face felt hot, the way it usually did when I was angry. I didn't like my mom telling me that. I didn't like having to be friends with someone I wasn't sure I liked. It was like having to eat hot cereal in the morning even when it didn't taste good. Before I knew it, the words slipped out. "If I was with Dad, I wouldn't have to see Perry again."

My mom grabbed her stomach as if I had hit her. I ran to her and buried my head in the apron she was wearing. I didn't want to see her face.

"I'm sorry," I said, and I was. "I'll be nice to Perry. I promise."

Inside I was thinking about my dad in New York City and that he wanted me. And I was thinking about my mom wanting me, too. I didn't think Perry would understand.

6

Everything was perfect for Perry. His father came down to the shore every weekend to spend time with him. He always brought Perry something from his clothing store: a new jacket, a baseball hat, a bright yellow shirt. They were always going out to dinner together, or to the amusement park, or to the movies. They'd laugh a lot, too, Perry and his father and mother. I tried not to listen. It bothered me. It never did before, when my dad was here.

Perry liked to play tennis and my mom had passes for any of the boarders who wanted to use the town tennis courts. It was a good walk — about a mile away.

"Come on," Perry said one cloudy day when it wasn't any good to go to the beach. "Let's go over and play tennis."

I remembered my promise to be nice to him. "Sure," I said and took my racket from the closet. We didn't talk much on the way to the tennis courts. Perry played a good game and I wasn't too bad. We hit the ball back and forth for a while. Then, right in the middle of a serve, Perry started laughing.

"Hey, look! There's that dog." He was pointing behind me. I turned around and there was Swimmer, playing with the extra tennis balls. He was having a grand old time throwing them up in the air and running after them.

"I guess he followed us here," I said, as if Swimmer were just any old stray dog.

I hit a ball to Perry to get his mind off Swimmer. Then I saw the red van from the animal shelter pull around the corner. I worried about that van from the first day I saw Swimmer. It came around about once a month, picking up stray dogs. Sometimes, someone would call and the red van would pull up on the block to get some cats that were starving in the bushes. I always felt sorry for the animals, but I knew starving was worse.

"You can't feed all the strays," my mom would say.

There was the red van now, going slowly around the outside of the tennis courts. My stomach turned over as I watched it.

"Hey, hit the ball," Perry called from the other side of the net.

I wasn't interested in the ball. I just watched

Swimmer jumping and running on the grass while the van kept going around the block. Then it stopped and a man got out. He walked across the grass toward the tennis court. Perry saw him, too, and came over to my side of the net.

"Whose dog is that?" the man asked. He was tall and had wide shoulders.

It was a long time before I answered. I felt Perry's eyes on me, almost burning into the back of my neck. When the man started to walk toward Swimmer, I shouted, "He's mine."

That stopped the man. He turned back to me. "You know he has to have a collar and license. You can't let him go running around town like that, son. Eventually he'll get picked up."

I nodded, not looking back at Perry. Then I ran toward Swimmer. "Come here, boy. I'll take you home."

The man left us on the tennis court and finally the van drove away.

"He's your dog?" Perry said, putting his racket down on the ground.

"Yeah," I mumbled.

"But what about that no-pets rule in your house?"

I knew he was thinking about his mother's cat. He looked angry, as if I had done something to her.

"That's for the people who live in the house," I

said. I was tired of always having to play the landlady's son. Being the landlady's son meant I had to take orders all day from the people who rented the rooms, and I had to pretend I didn't mind. I decided it should mean something good for a change. "Since we own the house," I said, "I can have a dog."

Perry got very quiet, as if he was thinking. Then he said, "My mom sure misses Pudgy. He hates staying at the vet's on the weekends when Dad comes down. Poor Pudgy, he hates being in a cage."

Perry looked at me as if he was blaming me for the whole thing. "It isn't my fault you have to send your cat away," I said. "Maybe your mother should try to find a place where they let you have pets." Actually when I thought about it, it seemed like a pretty good idea. The Harrises could have their cat and I could get rid of Perry.

"My mother likes this place," Perry said. "She says she comes back here because of the pool. There isn't another pool in any of the other boardinghouses. She doesn't like the beach that much." Then Perry got a funny look in his eyes, as if he had just figured something out.

"Does your mother know about the dog?" he asked.

I wished he hadn't asked that question. If he

hadn't, it would have been okay. But once he did, I was sure he would tell if I didn't make him understand that he better not. The only way I knew how to make him understand was to jump on him, and pin him down to the ground.

Perry was bigger than I was and put up a good fight. Swimmer didn't know what was happening. He stood over us, whimpering and licking our faces whenever he could as we rolled around.

Even though Perry was bigger and probably much stronger, I wanted to win more. While I was wrestling him around, I was thinking about my dad, and that got me angry. I was thinking about how happy we had been a few years ago and how happy Perry was now with his parents, and that got me angrier. I kept thinking about how nothing was ever going to be the same and how much I needed Swimmer. Finally I made Perry promise not to tell anyone about Swimmer.

I didn't really hurt him because I wasn't the type who enjoyed hurting someone else. But he was mad at me. I realized later it was because I didn't trust him. But I wasn't trusting anybody then. Perry walked home alone and Swimmer and I went back to the basement. I was tired and fell asleep on the rug with him. It wasn't a good sleep. I wasn't sure about Perry's promise. I knew he was angry and I knew promises could be broken.

"I'll always be with you," my dad had promised when I asked him once if he would ever go away.

Well, that one had been broken. I didn't think my dad would ever do that to me, so I didn't expect anything better from Perry.

Every day now I had a list of things to worry about. I'd go to Swimmer in the basement and then I'd worry whether the guy in the red van would find him or whether Perry would tell my mother that I had a dog, or whether Swimmer would just leave one day, like my dad.

I'd go to the beach and instead of watching the waves and the fishing boats, I'd think about my dad wanting me, and my mom wanting me. I felt like the town I grew up in wasn't my home anymore. I felt like I didn't belong anywhere. Days would go by without my finding something to feel good about.

"Don't you feel well?" my mother asked one day. I was sitting by the edge of the pool just staring at the leaves lying at the bottom. She felt my head.

"You don't have a fever," she said. "Maybe it's the heat."

It had been over ninety-eight degrees for five days and everyone was sleeping outside. Our boarders slept on the lounge chairs around the

51

pool and on the front porch at night. Some people slept on the boardwalk and on the sand by the water. Nobody was talking much, and if they did say something, it was usually not very nice.

"Don't bother me, Skip." Mr. Jasper waved me away. "No stories today. It's too hot."

Mom put me in bed with a cool sheet over me. She put some ice water by the bed. "Stay out of the sun today, Skip. You'll feel better tomorrow."

I didn't think so. Perry would still be there tomorrow, hanging over me like a big plant ready to fall on my head.

While I lay in bed, I reached over for the pitcher of ice water. There was a piece of paper on the table and it stuck to the bottom of the pitcher. I picked it off and read it. I wished I hadn't.

"I don't care if you take me to court," it read. "You won't get Skip. He's happy in this town. He's happy with me. You were the one who decided to leave. Don't destroy our family. We are a family, Skip and Paul and me."

I put the note back on the bureau and turned over under the cool sheets. It didn't seem like my problems would ever end. I wanted to stay in bed forever. The more I thought about it, the better I liked the idea.

But then I remembered Swimmer. As much as I wanted to disappear, I knew I had to take care of him. I crept out of bed, got dressed, and ran over to spend an hour with him.

Swimmer was the best friend I had now. I spent a lot of time with him, and a lot of time on Main Street walking by my dad's old office. Now and then I'd pretend he was still working there, and I was waiting outside for him.

I also ate a lot of doughnuts. The Donut Shop was one of my dad's favorite stops after lunch. I pretended he would be dropping in any minute.

"How's your dad?" the doughnut man asked every time I stopped in.

"Terrific," I answered. It seemed the best thing to say under the circumstances.

I noticed there was a sign up in The Donut Shop about the big swim-in taking place the last week in August. Every year, the winter people would hold a swim-in, just for themselves. It was hard to believe that August was here already, and that in a couple of weeks, school would be starting.

"Come join the swim-in," the sign read. "For residents of Bay City only." The sign meant the summer would soon be over, and Bay City would again belong to the winter people.

I loved the swim-in. Dad and I hadn't missed one since I was about five years old. He'd miss this one, and I didn't feel much like going by myself.

I stood there for a long time feeling sad about that, until I remembered Swimmer. Boy, would he ever be great in a swim-in. The only problem was, he wasn't a resident. I didn't have a license for him. Until he was mine, really mine, I knew I'd have to forget all about entering him in the swim-in.

I couldn't forget about making Swimmer mine. I wanted to own him. I wanted him to be a part of my family. I wanted everyone in town to know that Swimmer was my dog. I think Swimmer wanted that as much as I did.

7

I guess it was about mid-August when I began thinking how unfair it was, having to help out all summer when I could have been having fun. And then I thought about how nice it might be in New York City. There wouldn't be any boarding-house to keep clean, or any boarders ordering me around.

I bet my dad had a real neat apartment. If I was there during the summer, I could just watch television, or go to work with him sometimes. We could go to the movies and do all kinds of things.

I began to think more and more about that. Every time my mother called, "Skip, bring in the wash," or, "Skip, help me pull this hose over to the garden," or, "Skip, take the trash cans out front," I felt my skin grow hot. Didn't she know I didn't have to stay there? Didn't she know I could leave if I wanted to? My dad wanted me with him. Didn't she know that?

I wanted to remind her but there never seemed

to be much time for us to talk. Then came the amusement park night, and that just about did it.

Perry and I had been staying away from one another ever since the day at the tennis court. Mom didn't notice because Perry's father came down on vacation and Perry was spending a lot of time with his family. But one afternoon she came over by the pool, where I was taking a late swim.

"Skip, Perry's parents have invited you to go with them to the amusement park," she said. "It's their treat. They'll be going home soon."

Not soon enough for me, I thought. "I don't want to go," I answered. There was Swimmer to feed yet, and I wanted to be with him.

"Please go for me," my mother said. It had been a hot day and her hair was falling in her eyes. She had a tray of cool drinks she was bringing to the boarders sitting around the pool. I decided it was no time to give her more trouble. But I knew it was the last time I was going to be told what to do when it came to Perry.

I had to feed Swimmer first so I told my mom I wanted to get some gum at Charlie's store. I did. I didn't really want the gum, but I didn't feel good about lying to my mom, either. Buying the gum made me feel better. Then I went over to

Swimmer, who was still wet from his late afternoon swim.

"Boy, I sure wish I could have been swimming with you," I told him. I hugged him real tight. It was six o'clock and I could feel the sun getting weaker. I knew that soon there wouldn't be any sun at all at six o'clock. The days would be short. Then the shore would become windy and cold and dark. I looked at Swimmer, and his golden hair shining in the sun. I stared back at his trusting eyes. The basement wouldn't be warm enough in the winter. I just couldn't leave him there.

Maybe, if I couldn't keep Swimmer because of the boardinghouse, well, maybe, I thought, I could go to New York City with Swimmer. I didn't even see Perry until he was right by my side.

"So this is where you keep your dog," he said, standing there with his arms crossed and a very satisfied look on his face. "I wondered where you were hiding him out."

I still don't really believe what happened next. I mean, I don't really know what happened to me. All I saw was Perry standing there, looking as if he was pretty happy about what he had just found out.

I felt that rubber band snap inside of me. I just couldn't take another thing going wrong. I started yelling at him, louder than I ever remembered yelling in my life. Swimmer got so scared he ran into the basement. Perry got so scared, he ran right through the bushes. They were thorny bushes and he wasn't being too careful about how he got to the other side.

When I finally stopped yelling, I stood there for a moment, alone in the backyard. And then I knew what I had to do.

I ran to the boardwalk. There was a pay phone hanging from a pole. I ran to it and dialed the operator. I asked for my dad's phone number, collect. I felt so good when I heard his voice.

"Dad, are you allowed to have a dog in your apartment?" That's what I asked him after he said hello and asked if anything was wrong. I guess my voice sounded sort of excited.

"Yes, son. Some of the people have pets here. Why?" I could hear him thinking through the quiet at the other end. Then his voice got soft. "Skip, do you want to come and live with me? You know I want you to."

Boy, my heart was beating fast. My mouth felt so dry and my hands got cold. I felt afraid, but I didn't know why. It was my father I was talking to. I think I was just afraid of his question.

"I just wanted to know about the pets, that's

all," I said. Then I hung up before he could ask me anything else.

When I got home, which was way after seven o'clock, my mother was waiting for me. She was angrier than I had ever seen her.

"They left without you," she said, leading me into the bungalow. "Perry came home all scratched up and bleeding. He had ripped his shirt but he wouldn't say where he had been or what he was doing."

That was a surprise to me. I thought for sure everyone would know about Swimmer by now.

"I have a feeling you had something to do with what he looked like." My mother was looking right into my eyes now. Her blue ones were angry and cold, as if she didn't know me at all. I was beginning to think I didn't know myself, either.

I just shrugged. She said, "Into bed." She couldn't say, "Into your room," the way she did in the winter, because I didn't have a room in the summer. I didn't argue. I didn't really mind. I just wanted to be alone.

Later that night, Mom came and sat on the edge of my bed. She had her blond hair pulled back in a ponytail. She looked like a little girl instead of a mom who owned a large boardinghouse.

"Skipper. I know this has been a difficult summer for you," she said.

I didn't answer. I felt the tears piling up inside. But I didn't want to cry because then I knew she would cry, too.

"But you know," she smiled and it was as if a little light went on in that dark room, "pretty soon, everyone here will be going home." She pushed the hair off my forehead and her hand was cool and soft. "Then we'll have the shore all to ourselves again . . . the pool and the boardwalk and the ocean. Remember how pretty the leaves look in the fall when they fly off the trees and scatter across the boardwalk? And then when the snow comes and you can take your sled down the hills near the bay. We can eat in all the restaurants without waiting in line and shop in all the stores and we will have the time again to take our long walks on the boardwalk before we go to bed at night."

It was the same speech Mom gave me every year. It usually made me feel better. This time it didn't. I guess it was because Dad wasn't in the speech this year.

Perry stayed out of my way the next day. I thought I would feel good about that, but I didn't. There was something nagging at me now. I didn't feel right about the way I had treated him. He could have gotten even by telling my mother about Swimmer. But he didn't. I wondered why. I wanted to ask him, but I was ashamed. I just didn't know how.

I decided I was really messing things up for my mother. If I kept on going this way, she wouldn't have anyone coming here next year. So, in my head, I made plans to leave — with Swimmer, of course.

I would wait another few weeks until the end of the summer, so I wouldn't leave Mom in the middle. Then I would tell her. Swimmer and I would go live with Dad. I'd make sure I'd find some water for Swimmer. I guessed even in New York City they had a lake or a pool. With me gone, my mother would have less trouble with the people in the house. I would tell her it was best for her. We would have a nice long talk.

Lately, she didn't have time to talk to me about anything. She had stopped reading poetry and stories at night. We didn't talk much at dinner, either. When I mentioned Dad, her face would grow cross. So I stopped talking about him and everything else that was on my mind.

I didn't tell her about the letter I got from Paul that day, either. I didn't open the letter all day. I waited until late afternoon. Then I ran to the beach and sat on one of the rocks on the jetty. When I read his letter, I felt we were having a visit together. It was as if Paul knew I needed him.

Dear Skipper,
I never thought I'd say this but I miss Bay City. You know it's funny, Skipper, how some things that are never important to you become important once you leave them. And, you know, there's not a good pizza in this whole town. I keep thinking about the pizza and the hoagies back home — you know, the big ones with all the hot peppers. And then the swing set. Now isn't that a dumb one, Skipper? But I keep thinking about that swing set right next to the ocean on that piece of sand and how when I used to swing real high the ocean seemed to be right beneath my feet.

Yesterday I was looking in one of those gift shops and they had some seashells and sand in a jar. It was a pretty kind of thing and I started thinking about the sand. Remember the castles we used to make, and how the water used to wash over them? I even remembered the time we lugged home a big log that had washed up during a storm and stuck it in front of the house. It used to be great after a storm when all that junk would come up on the beach and we'd go down and sort through it.

I miss that ocean, Skipper. Remember how we'd go running into it after school, clothes and all? Sometimes even in the winter, without Mom knowing, just to say we'd been swimming in the winter. When I talk about it here, no one understands. So you see, Skipper, how things change when you get away from them.

I can't wait to get home when my hitch is up, little brother. So you'd better get ready for one big swim in that ocean and a race you'll never forget.

Love,
Paul

P.S. I guess things are pretty dull there right now with all the grouches giving orders. But hold on until I can get there to help you out.

I put the letter back in the envelope. Then I looked around the beach to make sure nobody else was around. It was dinnertime for most people and the beach was practically empty. So I did just what I wanted to do. I ran up and down the beach, right near the ocean's edge, yelling as loud as I could. For the first time all day, I was happy.

8

One night my mom's best friend, Edna, came to supper. After we cleaned up and put away the dishes, I went to bed. I wasn't feeling very good. They sat outside in front of the bungalow and I could hear them talking.

"He's not sending me the support money on time," my mother told Edna. "I know he's holding back so that I'll let Skippy go live with him."

"He has no right to do that." Edna was mad at my dad. I could tell by the way her voice went up and down.

"He left you to live somewhere else. It wasn't your fault." Edna's voice turned soft and I knew she was trying to make my mother feel better.

"Maybe. Maybe not," my mother answered. "I know he hated the shore. He wasn't a shore person. He lived in the city all his life. He came here because of me. He never felt it was his home. I remember when we got married and came back from our honeymoon, Bob just stood there — it was winter — and he said, 'Is it always this empty?' " My mother's voice sounded as if it was mixed with crying.

"Now don't go blaming yourself, Sarah. You did everything you could to keep that marriage together."

"Maybe," my mother said, but she didn't sound so sure. "Sometimes I think, maybe we should have moved when my parents died and left us this place. Maybe I should have sold it and asked Bob where he wanted to live."

I lay there thinking what it would be like living somewhere else, away from the ocean and the seagulls that woke me up each morning with their talking. If the seagulls happened to be someplace else, there was this bird that took over their pole. Once in a while I saw him and I couldn't believe anything that small could have a voice so big.

I couldn't imagine living without the boardwalk to run down whenever I felt like it, or the beach. I wanted to tell my mom she was right to stay here. And I knew I had to stay here, too.

"The insurance on the house is due soon." My mother's voice was worried. "If Bob doesn't send me money soon, I don't know what I'll do."

I didn't sleep very well that night. Only a mean person would do what my dad was doing. But I knew he wasn't mean, or bad. Maybe he felt the way I did the day I started yelling at Perry. Maybe he just felt mixed up inside.

When I woke the next morning, my head hurt and my eyes were blurred. My cheeks felt hot and my stomach turned over each time I got out of bed.

"You've got one hundred and two," my mother said, staring at the thermometer with a worried look. "I'm going to call the doctor."

The doctor told Mom I should stay in bed, drink lots of juices, and not do any swimming all week. He said I probably had whatever was going around and in another day or two, I would be up on my feet again. He said to call if there was any change.

I lay there all day, knowing the clock was moving toward Swimmer's dinner hour.

From my bed I could see through the screen door over to the pool. Everyone was having a great time diving into the water. Perry was out there, too. It had been a good summer for swimming and sunbathing, and now that it was coming to an end, no one wanted to miss a minute of it. I saw Perry dive off the diving board and do a belly flop into the water. For a while he floated on one of the rubber tires my mother kept in the pool.

I still couldn't figure out why Perry hadn't told my mother about Swimmer. Or even his mother, who surely would have told my mother. Perry had kept my secret as if it was his secret, too. Almost as if he was a real friend, like Pete and Billy.

About every hour or so, I'd try out my legs. I'd get up from the cot, hold on to the side, and walk a little toward the refrigerator where I'd get some soda. That's about all the strength I had. I couldn't wait to lie down again. My stomach would start heaving and I'd break out in a sweat. I knew I wouldn't be able to make it around the corner to Swimmer.

Around four o'clock I was really getting scared. Half of me wanted to run out and tell my mom, who was sweeping up around the pool. But she would know that I was keeping Swimmer for my own. I knew she would point to that sign on the front wall, and then she would call the animal shelter and the red van would come to the abandoned house.

It was then that I knew something else. I was going to have to trust Perry. There was no one else around who could help me out. Pete and Billy were away. But Perry was right outside my window. I knew in about a half hour his mother would call him to come in for a shower. I knew Perry would leave the pool, go in the house, and about fifteen minutes later he would walk under my window toward the back clothesline where he always hung his wet bathing suit and towel.

I waited, sipping my soda, going carefully over the plan in my head so I would get it right. It was pretty difficult to concentrate with the fever working against me, but in a little while I heard a voice call from the top floor.

"Perry, it's time for your shower."

Perry didn't go in right away. I didn't blame him. The day was too perfect. He took two more dives off the edge of the pool and then swam from one end to the other three times. Then he grabbed his towel and ran up the steps of the back porch.

I waited, watching the clock. Five minutes went by . . . then ten, then fifteen, then twenty. I was beginning to get really worried when finally Perry came running down the porch steps, carrying his swimsuit and towel. I leaned over toward the screen window, which took all my strength because parts of my body were not listening to me that day. I waited. As he passed my window, I whispered loud enough so he could hear, but not loud enough for anyone else to hear. "Hey, Perry. Come here."

Perry stopped and looked around. The screen was dark and I guess he couldn't see my face right away. But then as he peered in my direction, he smiled and ran over. He pressed his face very close to the screen and put his hand over his forehead to see me better.

"Hey, Skip. I heard you were sick. How do you feel?"

"Okay," I answered. I had a big "I'm sorry" speech all ready for him, but I could tell by his voice he wasn't mad anymore. I decided to save the speech. Something else was more important and my head was hurting and I didn't think I was going to want to sit up for too much longer.

"Perry, I need your help. Swimmer needs food and water and I can't get to him. Would you help me?"

Perry could have made it real bad for me then. I knew I was in his hands. I leaned against the screen just looking at him, and feeling bad about how I had treated him all summer. It was one of those times when you realize how much you need someone. I needed Perry and he knew it.

"Where do you keep his food?" he asked.

"On a shelf in the basement. It's the only shelf there. But I'm not sure if there's any left."

"What if there isn't? What kind does Swimmer like?"

"The dry kind. Charlie will know. But then he has to drink a lot of water when he's done. Make sure you fill his water dish. I get the water in back of Charlie's."

"Okay," Perry answered.

"And listen," I said, remembering how Swimmer loved to play ball after his belly was full. "If you have a little extra time, could you just play a little ball with him?" I looked around my bedroom and realized I didn't know where the ball was. Sometimes I brought it home with me.

"Don't worry about it," Perry said. "Charlie has a whole bunch of them in a rack. I'll get Swimmer a new ball. I have enough money with me."

"Great," I said, wishing I could do something nice for Perry the way he was doing something nice for me. "He likes it when you scratch him under the neck and behind his ears after he eats. Don't be afraid if he jumps up on you all of a sudden and puts his paws up on your shoulders. It's his way of thanking you. Swimmer can really hug."

"I'll go over now," Perry whispered back. "Don't worry."

All I could manage was a weak "Thank you." The fever was taking away my energy.

I watched Perry run to the back clothesline and hang up his things. Then I heard his mother call. "Perry, hurry up. Your dinner's ready."

I pressed my face against the screen and strained my eyes. I saw Perry look back toward my window, then run down the steps, past the brick wall, and around the corner.

About fifteen minutes later, I heard Perry whisper, "Skip, are you there?"

"Yeah," I answered.

"I fed Swimmer and I gave him water. He's sleeping now."

"Thanks, Perry."

"I'll do it tomorrow, too. Don't worry."

"Thanks."

"Hurry up and get better."

"Right, Perry."

I slept good that night. Somewhere toward morning, I felt a coolness come over me and I knew the fever was leaving. But I still didn't feel well enough to get up.

The next day, I sat on the edge of the bed and walked around the room a little. I read some comic books and watched television.

Every couple of hours my mom would come in to give me more juice or soda, or feel my head. She always left a piece of toast on the bureau by my bed. It gave me a chance, lying there, to see how busy she really was. From the time she got up in the morning, until the time she went to bed at night, she was always doing something for someone in the house. I felt bad that I wasn't able to help her out. I knew she needed me to clean the pool, or sweep up at the end of the day, or do some shopping for one of the older people who didn't have a car. My mom was like that. She didn't have to shop for the boarders, but if they ran out of food and couldn't get to the food market, she'd run them over in our car, or have me take a trip to Charlie's.

I knew I was sick because even the boarders were worried about me.

Mrs. Patterson sent in a comic book and a bowl of chicken soup. "Keep up your strength, Skipper," she said when she came into my room. "That chicken soup will help you."

Old Mr. Cooperson, who didn't talk to anybody except when he wanted to complain, came in with a bag of lollipops. He pulled out a coloring book and crayons from a paper bag. "I didn't know if you were too old for this sort of thing," he said. "I used to like them when I was sick." He stayed awhile and colored in one of the pictures in the book.

It was sort of nice. It was like having a whole bunch of grandparents worrying about me. I didn't have any of my own around. My mother's parents died when I was very young and my father's parents lived in Florida. We only got to see them once a year. I began to think maybe some of these older people who came here for the summer wanted to be able to take care of someone, too. By the end of the day, there was a pile of comic books, crayons, three bags of lollipops, and a model airplane from Perry that I couldn't wait to put together.

Now that I knew Swimmer was being taken care of, I could sleep without tossing and turning. I missed him, though, and wondered if he was missing me, too. I knew it was important for Swimmer to know I hadn't deserted him. Maybe the way people had before me. I knew what it felt like to have someone walk out on you, and I wasn't sure Swimmer knew he could trust me not to do that.

9

It was very early on the third morning when I heard it. I was lying in bed, sort of half asleep, feeling certain that I would be able to get outside that day, when I heard this roar. It was like the top of the house had fallen in. I sat up in bed. I thought maybe it was thunder. When we get a storm at the shore, sounds bounce off the water and there's a roaring, rumbling noise that almost sounds like the one I heard then.

I looked outside. The sun was out. My mom was turning on the pool water. I looked at the clock. It was eight o'clock in the morning. When Mom came in, the noise was still going on.

I climbed out of bed and put on my shorts. "Mom, where's that noise coming from?"

She saw me getting dressed and smiled. "Oh honey, I'm glad you're back on your feet again. You had me so worried. I don't want you to do much yet. Take it easy for another day or two."

I asked her about the noise again.

"Oh that," she said. "They're finally tearing down that old house around the corner."

Well, you can imagine what happened then. I can hardly get it straight even thinking about it now. All I could think of was Swimmer in the basement of that house, and that house coming down on top of him. Just as my mom finished telling me about the abandoned house, Perry showed up at the window.

His face was pressed against the screen. "It's the house," Perry said. And he looked as worried as I was.

"What are they doing to it?" I wanted to scream.

"Tearing it to shreds. They've got all these big trucks and machines on the lot."

I went over to the window so Mom couldn't hear.

"What about Swimmer?" I whispered.

Perry shook his head. "I couldn't see him. I ran over there. When I went to get a newspaper at Charlie's, a whole bunch of people were standing on the sidewalk watching. You really can't see too much. Can you come out today?"

"Are you kidding? I've got to get over there. I'm almost dressed," I said, reaching for my sneakers.

"I'll wait for you outside. Hurry." Perry's voice was urgent.

"I've got to go over to that house," I told my mother. My hands were shaking as I tried to tie the laces on my sneakers. My mother told me I had to wear them because I was just getting over being sick.

"You're not going anywhere, young man." My mother sat me firmly back down on the bed. "You're still too weak. I want you to stay on the front porch. You can just miss that old house falling down."

"You don't understand — "

I couldn't finish what I had to say because the telephone rang. It was Mrs. Patterson. Her toilet had backed up and she needed Mom right away. As if that wasn't bad enough, Mrs. Apple blew the fuses again. All the electricity was off in the big house.

But all I could think of was Swimmer, Swimmer in the basement, and those cranes knocking the house down.

"I've got to get Swimmer." I was mumbling to myself and hoping Mom would just go over and fix the electricity. I didn't think I was talking that loud until my mother turned around and asked, "Who's Swimmer?"

Everything tumbled out then. It reminded me of what happens to the sand on the beach in a windstorm. It starts flying around and everything gets caught up in it. Well, that's what was happening to me. The boarders were waiting, my mother's questioning eyes were facing me, and Swimmer was in danger. I didn't have a chance to tell Mom about Swimmer the way I had hoped to, nice and calm and sweet. I told her while I was yelling about my dad leaving and how I felt about this whole rotten summer. I also put in something about the boarders bossing her around. I didn't mean for that to get in there. I ended by telling my mom that I wished she'd let the boarders know that since we owned the house, we could do things differently. And if we wanted to, we could have a dog.

Well, my mom just sat down on my bed. She looked as if someone had knocked the wind out of her. I thought for sure she was going to cry. I don't think I had ever yelled at her before. I thought maybe she would slap me. I felt I deserved it. I thought my heart would beat right out of my chest as I waited for her to do something, anything but just sit there as if she couldn't move.

Finally, she stood up and walked over to me. She put her hands on my shoulders and in one big sweep, took me inside her arms, the way she had when I was very small. She hugged me so hard, I almost couldn't breathe. But I didn't say anything. It felt too good.

"I'm sorry, Skippy," she said. "I didn't realize."

What happened after that, I remember very clearly.

"Come with me," she said. We marched right past Mrs. Apple and Mrs. Patterson and the other boarders who were standing around by the pool.

"What about my toilet?" Mrs. Patterson asked.

"And my hot plate. There's no electricity," Mrs. Apple called out to us.

"I'll fix the electricity but the rest will have to wait until I get back," my mother said firmly.

Mr. Grey caught her just as we were walking down the front steps.

"I'm all out of groceries," he said. "Do you think you could just run over to the store?"

"If I have time later," my mother answered. Her voice was very strong, the way I remembered it before my father left. "Right now my son needs me. I'm going to be busy all morning. When I get back, I'll deal with everything."

Mom put her arm around my shoulders and we walked down the street toward the abandoned house. Perry was running alongside us.

"He's okay. I'm sure he got out," he kept saying.

All I could hear was the house falling. When we got to the house there was a crowd standing in the street, staring. Everyone in town did that when anything unusual happened. If there was a

78

fire or someone got hurt or a swimmer was caught out in the ocean, everyone would stand along the boardwalk or in the street, watching. They were doing that now.

Old Charlie was there, too. He'd known my mother since she was a little girl.

"I've got to find out if Swimmer is in there," I begged her. I just couldn't stand there waiting with the rest of them until the whole house was destroyed.

"You mean that golden retriever you been feeding?" Charlie said, giving me a pretzel from his bag. I passed it on to Perry. I didn't feel much like eating.

"You saw him?" I waited. Charlie never rushed when he talked, especially when he was eating pretzels.

"Sure did. He left as soon as the cranes pulled up. Ran off scared as anything. I tried to catch him. I knew you were taking care of him. I tried," Charlie said.

I knew he meant it. I also knew I hadn't fooled Charlie, just the way no one else in town could fool him.

Standing there, I felt good and bad all at once. I felt good because I knew Swimmer was safe, but bad because I didn't know if I would ever see him again.

"I've got to find him," I told Mom and Perry. "He's going to think I don't care about him anymore. He'll think because I didn't show up for those couple of days, that I stopped needing him. I know he feels that. He probably thinks I forgot all about him."

I thought about my dad when I said that. I wondered if that's how he felt about me.

"Don't worry, honey," my mom said. "We're going to look all over this town until we find him."

We searched through all the streets of Bay City, even across Star Lake bridge. Charlie, Perry, Mom, and me and anyone else who happened to walk by and find out that our dog was missing. That's how Mom put it whenever she asked anyone about a golden retriever.

"We've lost our dog," she said. "Have you seen it anywhere?"

But Swimmer was gone. He wasn't in the water swimming, not on the beach playing, not under the boardwalk sniffing the garbage cans, not walking on the boardwalk, not anywhere in town.

"Do you think I'll ever see him again?" I asked Perry as we walked up one street and down another.

"Sure," he said, trying to make me feel better. "Swimmer just got scared. You know how it is. He's probably running around somewhere trying to figure out what all those trucks were doing at his house. Once he calms down, he'll come back."

I knew what it was like to feel that scared. I remember once there was a terrible storm at the shore. The ocean was up to our house and the boardwalk was washed out in places. The roads were flooded and we had to leave our house and stay in the school. I felt safe there and when the storm was over I forgot all about it.

Maybe Swimmer would do that, too. Maybe he'd run around until he stopped being afraid and then he'd come back to see what I thought about it. I'd stroke his head and scratch him under the neck and tell him not to be afraid anymore. Maybe.

10

We had plenty of help looking for Swimmer. Even some of the boarders from our house went out when they found out what had happened.

We drove to the police station and asked if they had picked up any dogs or knew of any that had been hit by cars during the last couple of hours. I felt my heart pounding real loud while I waited until they checked their records.

"No," the policeman answered. "But leave a description and a phone number and we'll keep an eye out for him."

We visited the ASPCA and looked in the cages. All the dogs looked so sad, as if they were expecting to see someone they knew. There were some dogs that looked like Swimmer, but they didn't have that something special in their eyes or that funny grin. I knew I'd know Swimmer when I saw him.

We drove back along by the boardwalk and along Main Street and even went up and down the long streets that lead to the beach again. I never realized there were so many houses with backyards and sheds and porches. There were so many places Swimmer could be hiding.

Perry kept trying to make me feel better, telling me all kinds of reports about missing animals that he'd seen in the newspapers or on tv.

"I heard a story about a dog who was missing for four weeks," he said. "One day he came back to his house. The people found him right in their backyard. I read that dogs can find their way back to their homes no matter how far away they wander. I bet you Swimmer will just show up at your house one day."

I didn't believe Perry and he looked like he didn't believe himself, either.

Well, Mrs. Patterson's toilet didn't get fixed that day because we didn't get home until suppertime.

Later that night, Perry and I sat on the rocking chairs on the front porch talking. I knew it was time for the "I'm sorry" speech. Perry had been out looking with me all day. I knew I had to give him something back.

"Perry, I'm sorry I was so mean this summer," I said. "It was just a time when nothing turned out right. Know what I mean?"

"Yeah," he answered. "I know. I'm sorry about

your dad leaving. I heard my mother and father talking about it. My mom says maybe we won't come back next summer, but I hope we do. It's just that she hates leaving our cat behind. I do, too."

"I understand how she feels," I said. I had lost Swimmer and it felt like I had a big hole in my chest somewhere near my heart that wouldn't fill up until I had Swimmer back with me again.

Perry smiled. "Sometimes I think that cat is my best friend. I can always depend on him. And he's always glad to see me when I come home from school. He sits right on the chair next to me when I'm eating."

Even though Perry had been coming down for a couple of summers, I felt I was just getting to know him. He was being real honest with me, so I thought it was a good time to ask him something that was on my mind.

"Why didn't you tell my mom about Swimmer?" I asked.

"I don't snitch on my friends," he answered. Then he took out his deck of cards and we began to play war on the card table under the small light on the porch. That's about what Pete and Billy would have said.

The next morning I got up early. I felt well enough again for a swim in the ocean. It wouldn't be much fun without Swimmer, though. I was hoping he'd had a chance to think over what happened, and I knew if he cared for me the way I cared for him, he'd come back. He was a smart dog and I knew he'd remember where we met.

As I ran up the ramp of the boardwalk, I almost couldn't look at the beach. I knew if he wasn't there, he wouldn't be, ever again. It was like that. I knew it inside. I looked quickly over the sand. A few dogs were running around, searching the garbage cans for food, but not Swimmer. I ran down to the edge of the water. It was calm, like a lake, and warm around my toes.

I dove under a wave. And then I did what I did the first time Swimmer and I met. I swam back and forth, closing my eyes and hoping that it would happen again. Back and forth, back and forth. I hoped and waited and squeezed my eyes shut against the salty water. Somewhere during the fifth time back and forth I sensed it, that feeling that someone was swimming with me. I opened my eyes and there was Swimmer, grinning just like I was.

This time Swimmer and I went back to my house. We walked right past the sign that said NO PETS, right into the bungalow, and right up to my mom, who smiled, bent down, and hugged Swimmer.

I wanted to stay around while Swimmer and

Mom got to know one another, but I had something important to do.

"I'll be right back," I told her, leaving Swimmer lapping up her attention. I ran up to the boardwalk telephone and dialed the operator. Then I called my dad, collect. I wasn't sure about what I had to do before. Now I knew.

"Hey, Skip. I've missed you. How you doing?"

"Okay, Dad." I decided not to waste any time because long distance calls are expensive.

"Dad, I'm staying here. Mom needs me. She's got this whole house to take care of and I know she couldn't do it without me." Knowing that made me feel important.

There was a long silence at the other end. "Skippy, I miss you so."

"I'll come to New York City to visit, right after the summer season ends," I promised him. "I'll come on weekends."

"Would you, Skip? I'd love that. I'll talk to your mother about that."

I knew I had to say everything and I felt we could talk to each other now, man to man. Somehow this past summer had made me feel older than ten.

"Mom needs money, Dad. The insurance is due."

There was another long pause. "I'm sorry, Skip.

I didn't mean to hurt both of you. I'll send her a check tonight."

I hung up feeling better than I'd felt all summer. I didn't want to cost Dad too much money by staying on the phone to tell him how good I felt when Mom let everyone wait because I needed her. I didn't have the time to tell him about how Charlie closed his store for an hour so he could help us look for Swimmer. I didn't want to tell him how suddenly I looked at the ocean and the beach and I knew I never wanted to leave it. I didn't have time to tell him about Perry and me and how we had become friends.

I would tell him all about it on the weekends when we were together.

The next day, some of our boarders collected in little groups, whispering and talking to one another in front of our house.

It was Perry's mother who finally said what everyone was thinking, but I didn't hold it against Perry. He was standing by me and Swimmer, and I knew someone had to say it.

"I don't understand how you can have a dog," she said to my mother, "with that sign hanging on the wall in front of the house."

My mother, who wasn't very tall, seemed to

grow a few inches when she answered. "That sign," she said slowly so that each word was heard by everyone standing on the porch and around the steps, "is for the people who live in my house during the summer. It is not for the landlady and her son."

I could have sworn I saw Swimmer grin when she said that. Then Perry and Mom and Swimmer and I got in the car and drove off up the block. We were on our way to get Swimmer a license and then enter him in the Bay City Swim-in. After all, he was a resident now and would be here when the summer people went back to live in their own houses.

Thinking back on it, it wasn't such a bad summer after all. Perry and I had become friends and I had gotten to know my brother better. He is already making plans to paint the outside of our house when he comes home and he seems real happy about it. I don't have to tell you how good that makes Mom feel.

Swimmer didn't win the Bay City Swim-in but he came pretty close. He was one of the first ten to finish and the only dog to compete and win Honorable Mention. Next year may not be so easy. I hear a lot of people are going to enter their dogs.

Maybe the best thing that happened, though, had to do with the NO PETS sign. It hung in front of our house all winter. Mom had a funny look on her face every time she looked at it. Then one day, I saw her standing in front of it pulling it off. She threw the sign in a trash can by the curb.

"I guess as long as people take care of their animals, and they don't disturb anyone else, it wouldn't hurt to take a few people in who have pets. I know how we'd feel without Swimmer," she said.

Swimmer must have understood, because he stretched out and gave her one of his long hugs.